SUNNY'S TOW TRUCK SAVES THE DAY!

By **ANNE MARIE PACE**

Illustrated by **CHRISTOPHER LEE**

Abrams Appleseed
New York

Pack the cooler!
Picnic day!
Nine o'clock.
We're on our way.

We pile into the minivan.
The crowd's too big for Pop's sedan.

But halfway there . . .

THUMP-BUMPTY . . . SPLAT!

What's going on? Our tire's flat!

Get the spare.
Let's check the trunk.

The spare's flat, too?
Our hopes are sunk.

What to do?
Who can assist?
Lots of helpers
on this list!

Sunny's Towing will be great.
And now we simply have to wait.

It's nine thirty. Did you call her?
There she is! No, that's a hauler.

Ten o'clock. Is that her truck?
Just a pickup. Out of luck.

It's ten thirty. Traffic's growing.
Trucks work hard, but not at towing.
Cranes are lifting, pavers paving.
Diggers digging, workers waving.

Call back Sunny. "Coming soon?"
"Very busy. Could be noon."

In the distance, we see fire.
Situation could be dire.

See that cruiser zip away?
Officers must not delay.

Sirens screaming, horns are blowing.
Engines rushing, none are slowing.

Tractor-trailers, rough and rumbly.
Concrete mixers, tough and tumbly.

Dump trucks filled with piles of muck.
But no tow truck. We are stuck.

Sunny said it
might be noon.

Ten 'til. Five 'til.
Must be soon.

Then Sunny
and her truck
draw near.

Thank goodness, she is finally here!

Sunny tows us to her crew.
They know exactly what to do.

Patch the tires, fill with air.
Now we can drive anywhere!

But our picnic food has vanished!
While we waited, we were famished.
No tomatoes or pastrami.
No potatoes, no salami!

Sunny has a brilliant scheme.

She leads us to the best ice cream!

Off to the park. No more delay.
Still a perfect picnic day!

For Sofia —A. M. P.

For Kristine —C. L.

Cataloging-in-Publication Data has been applied for
and may be obtained from the Library of Congress.

Library of Congress Control Number 2018013949
ISBN 978-1-4197-3191-4

Printed and bound in China
10 9 8 7 6 5 4 3 2 1

For bulk discount inquiries, contact
specialsales@abramsbooks.com.

ABRAMS The Art of Books
195 Broadway, New York, NY 10007
abramsbooks.com